THE
EEN
H

Margaret Mahy

ILLUSTRATED BY Steven Kellogg

ARTHUR A. LEVINE BOOKS

AN IMPRINT OF SCHOLASTIC INC.

"Look at yourself!" cried his mother. "You're covered with dust and dead spiders."

"But I was sneaking up on pirates," cried Sammy. "How can I have adventures and stay clean?"

"Just forget about adventures for the moment," said his mother. "Your grandma's coming, so stay clean for once."

Next door, Mr. Trottingham had just come home from the flea market. A speedboat shone, sleek and scarlet, on the trailer.

Five minutes later Sammy's father came home. He had something on his trailer too.

"*Ha! Ha!* HA-HA! Have a happy bath!" Terry Trottingham shouted through the hole in the hedge. "*We're* going to whiz over the waves in our wonderful speedboat."

Sammy watched his father connect the bath to the pipes and stepped HARD on one clawed foot.

Toot! Toot! honked the Trottingham horn as they set off for the seashore.

But just at that moment, Sammy heard the bath give a gurgle as if it were laughing.

He thought he saw it scratching itself with one of its strange claw-feet. He blinked and looked again.

No! The bath was standing as still as baths usually stand. "Now, get into that bath and wash yourself," his mother was saying.

Sammy tried to make his first soaking as adventurous as possible. Putting on his swimming suit, his snorkel, and water wings, he poured a few drops of foaming soap into the water, then lay back among the bubbles, singing a little song.

The owl and the pussycat sped to sea

In a beautiful pea-green bath.

Leaping the lawn,

Hopping over the hedge,

And prancing along the path.

The bath jiggled. Sammy pretended not to notice. He kept
on singing. The bath jumped. Sammy sang even more loudly.

The bathroom window was wide open. Sammy could hear in the far, far distance the Trottinghams carrying on at the shore. He sang on.

Then, all in a minute, the bath was off and away.

It bounded through the back door,

leaped across the lawn, hopped over the hedge,

and made for the wide, wide ocean.

People gasped. Then they cheered and waved their towels.
SPLASH! A warm summer wave swept up and over the
Trottingham twins as the green bath dived into the green sea.

SPLASH, again! Off went the bath.

Mermaids lifted heads of seaweed hair. "Boy in a bath! Boy in a bath!" they sweetly sang.

A sea serpent appeared. "Race you!" it roared.

"Three times around Treasure Island."

Soon the Island was right in front of them. On the beach a whole boatload of buccaneers was hard at work, digging for treasure.

"A bath like that is real treasure," muttered the captain.

"Buccaneers need baths even more than boys do.

Board it quickly! Prepare to wash!"

"I'm on your side,"
hissed the sea serpent
to Sammy.

Then began a wonderful
bath-and-buccaneer battle.

The buccaneers had swords, but Sammy bewildered
them with bubbles and baffled them with soapsuds.

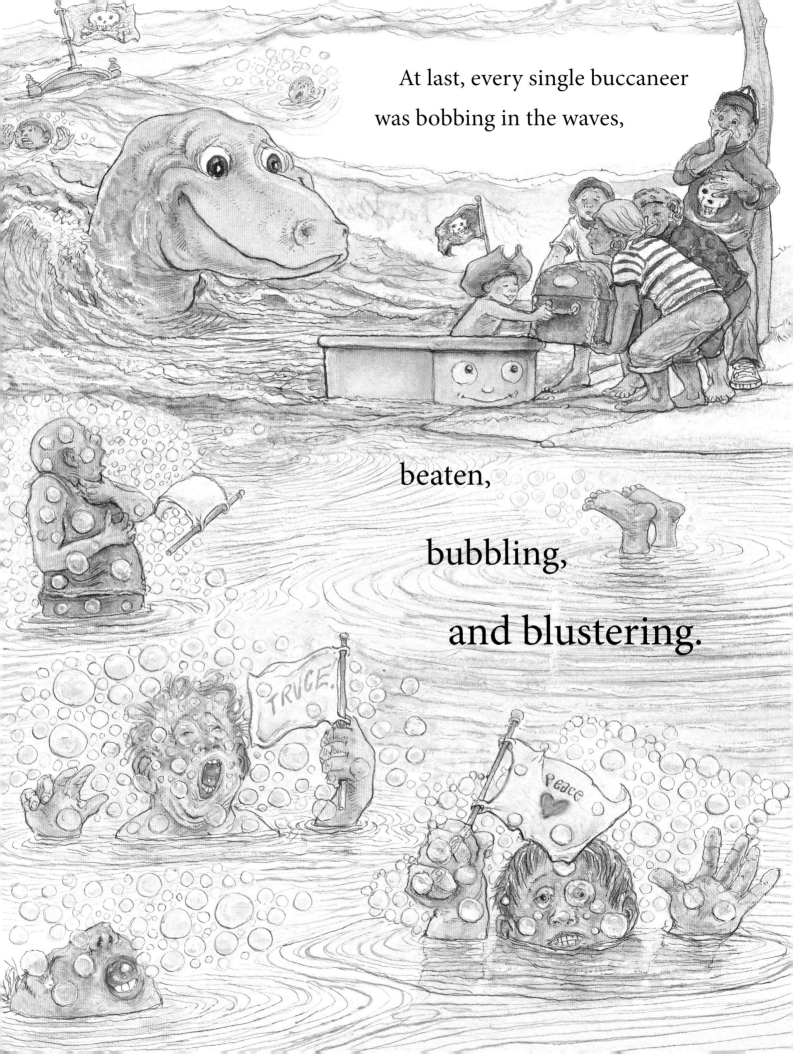

At last, every single buccaneer

was bobbing in the waves,

beaten,

bubbling,

and blustering.

Then the bath turned back toward the beach once more. "Come back soon, Sammy!" shouted the sea serpent.

The bath enjoyed the wildest water.

It bobbed! It bounded!

It whisked up waves that rock-and-rolled
every other boat in the bay.

Reaching the beach safely,

the bath scampered back the way it came

and settled itself into the bathroom once more . . .

. . . just as Sammy's mother walked in without knocking, the way mothers sometimes do.

"My goodness!" she said. "What's gone on in here!!"

Sammy scrambled out of the bath and gave his mother
the sort of smacking kiss a pirate in a good mood might
give. Then, wrapping himself in a towel, he began to arrange
the treasure on the window ledge.

As the water gurgled down the drain, it certainly

sounded as if that bath were laughing, loud and clear.

Text copyright © 2013 by Margaret Mahy
Illustrations copyright © 2013 by Steven Kellogg

All rights reserved. Published by Arthur A. Levine Books, an imprint of Scholastic Inc., *Publishers since 1920*.
SCHOLASTIC and the LANTERN LOGO are trademarks and/or registered trademarks of Scholastic Inc.

LIBRARY OF CONGRESS CATALOGING-IN-PUBLICATION DATA

Mahy, Margaret.
The green bath / Margaret Mahy ; illustrated by Steven Kellogg. — 1st ed.   p.   cm.
Summary: Sammy's mother tells him to forget about adventures and get cleaned up for his grandmother's
visit, but the new bathtub Sammy's father brought home seems determined to have an adventure of its own.
ISBN 978-0-545-20667-9 (hardcover : alk. paper)
[1. Bathtubs—Fiction. 2. Adventure and adventurers—Fiction. 3. Baths—Fiction.]
I. Kellogg, Steven, ill. II. Title.   PZ7.M2773Gt 2013   [E] —dc23   2012013239

10 9 8 7 6 5 4 3 2 1   13 14 15 16 17

First edition, July 2013
Printed in Malaysia 108

The text type was set in 18-pt. Minion Pro Regular. The display type was set in Bovine Poster Regular.
The art for this book was created using a mixed medium combination of pencils, watercolor, colored inks, and acrylics.
Book design by Marijka Kostiw